Would you rather Christmas for youngsters

Would you rather book for youngsters Christmas release

By

Flora Mitchell

Copyright@2022

Table of Contents

INTRODUCTION

How much time enjoyed with family and other dear companions makes Christmas so unique. Because everyone is congregating in a single location, this is also a great time to engage in some lighthearted games. The game *Would You Rather Christmas For Youngsters*, which has a festive theme, is straightforward, and can be played by anyone, perfectly exemplifies this point. Playing Christmas This or That or would you rather Christmas for youngsters is simple. Simply inquire about each person's preference at the table. After everyone has made their decision, you are welcome to discuss the issue together.

What are some good questions to ask about Christmas?

Family, food, and festivities take center stage during the holidays. Even though all of the parties and gatherings are exciting, they can also cause stress and boredom. Spend some time getting to know this game of 150 Would You Rather Christmas Questions for Youngsters.

Chapter 1

Which is your favorite holiday meal? turkey or ram?

Do you prefer to consume only holiday foods for a week or listen to holiday music?

Do you prefer to make gifts yourself or buy them?

Which do you prefer, receiving or giving?

Do you prefer to contribute financially or volunteer your time at a shelter for the homeless?

During the holiday season, do you prefer to string only white lights or any other color?

Do you prefer to travel or spend Christmas at home?

On Christmas Day, which do you prefer, the beach or the mountains?

Would you rather have your child's father be Clark Griswold from National Lampoon's Christmas Vacation or George Bailey from It's a Wonderful Life?

This holiday season, would you rather only receive cards or only gifts?

Do you like to open gifts on Christmas morning or on Christmas Eve?

Do you like to wrap presents or shop for presents?

Do you like to celebrate with just your immediate family or with your entire extended family?

Do you prefer to spend Christmas with your family wearing ugly Christmas sweaters or matching pajamas?

Which artist would you rather listen to—Mariah Carey or Bing Crosby?

Do you like to celebrate the holidays with your entire family at once or over the course of the month?

Funny questions about Christmas

Which do you prefer, an elf suit or a Santa suit to wear around town for a day?

The Rockefeller Tree in New York City or a palm tree on a beach adorned with Christmas lights?

Do you prefer ice skating or skiing?

Which would you rather consume, a jello mold or an entire fruitcake?

Which do you prefer better, eggnog or hot chocolate?

Do you prefer to participate in a White Elephant gift exchange or a Secret Santa?

Which book, The Night Before Christmas or The Christmas Story from the Bible, do you prefer to read on Christmas Eve?

Do you prefer to listen to a Christmas choir or sing in the choir?

You can choose to give 12 Christmas gifts or do 12 random acts of kindness.

Do you prefer a real or a fake Christmas tree?

Do you prefer to decorate the tree with handmade or store-bought ornaments?

Do you prefer to participate in a gingerbread house competition or host a cookie swap in your neighborhood?

Which do you prefer to view the Christmas lights from, a horse-drawn wagon or your car?

Would you rather have Christmas cookies delivered to you from a neighbor instead?

Could you rather watch a Christmas film or read Christmas picture books?

Do you prefer to never eat candy canes or Christmas cookies again?

Do you prefer to decorate gingerbread houses or Christmas cookies?

You can ride the Polar Express as a passenger or drive Santa's sleigh.

Which do you prefer, the Grinch or Who in Who-ville?

Do you prefer to fall asleep quickly so that you can open presents or to spend the entire night trying to see Santa?

Would you rather receive ten smaller gifts or one large one?

Would you rather melt like Frosty or have a red nose that flashes red when you're hungry, like Rudolph, when you get warm?

Which would you prefer to give—your toys or cash from your savings account?

Do you prefer to be aware of what you are getting under the tree or be surprised?

On Christmas Day, would you rather go swimming or skiing?

Do you like to rise and shine from the get-go Christmas Day or snooze?

When you flush, do you want your toilet to play "Oh Holy Night" or "Jingle Bells"?

Do you prefer to spend Christmas at Disney World without any presents or at home with gifts?

Do you prefer to visit Santa at the mall or write a letter to him?

Christmas Edition which game do you prefer

Which do you prefer to use as ornaments on your Christmas tree—an angel or a star?

Do you prefer to slowly or quickly open all of your presents?

Which do you prefer, Mrs. Clause or the head elf?

Which would you rather be—an animal in the Nativity scene or a reindeer pulling Santa's sleigh?

Would you rather receive only the gold, frankincense, and myrrh that the wiseman brought, or would you rather receive only clothes, underwear, and socks?

Which would you rather do in December—eating a candy cane each day or opening a small present each day?

Do you prefer to make a list and only receive five gifts, or do you prefer to receive more gifts if you do not make a list?

Which character in the Nutcracker would you rather portray, a soldier or a mouse?

Would you rather keep your birthday the same or celebrate it on Christmas Day?

Which character would you rather portray in a Christmas pageant—an animal or a wiseman?

Do you like to live in a gingerbread house or to decorate one?

Do you prefer to spend the entire year listening to holiday music or to be on the naughty list this year?

Would you rather work for Santa than be the Grinch during the day?

Could you fairly go to Bethlehem or the North Pole?

Do you prefer to participate in a live nativity or a Christmas play?

Fun Christmas questions for holiday

Which holiday decoration would you prefer?

Which would be more convenient—before or after Thanksgiving?

Which date—February 1 or December 25—is more convenient for you to remove Christmas decorations?

Do you prefer to attend the work Christmas party or spend the night alone at home?

If you're the kind of person who likes to shop until you drop, here's a free tracker to help you keep track of your Christmas shopping!

You would rather cook the holiday meal or do the dishes.

Which do you prefer—something fun or something useful?

Do you prefer to be trapped in the snow with your in-laws or stuck in an airport?

Could you rather invest less energy shopping yet spend more cash? Or would it be preferable for you to devote more time to looking for the best deals?

Which do you prefer, Love Actually or White Christmas?

Do you prefer Gremlins or Die Hard? My husband claims that these films count as Christmas films. Would you rather hang Christmas lights or help your neighbors shovel snow?

Do you prefer a chocolate advent calendar or a boozy one?

When you go to karaoke, do you prefer to sing "Santa Baby" or "All I want for Christmas is you"?

Do you prefer to act as an actor in a Hallmark Christmas movie or dance with the Rockettes?

Do you prefer to have your holiday bonus revoked by your boss or to have your tongue frozen solid?

Do you like a Christmas tree in every room or a lot of lights around the house?

Chapter 2
Would You like holiday school questions

A talking reindeer or a talking snowman, which would you rather spend the day with?

Which do you prefer for Christmas—a kitten or a puppy?

Would you rather have to sing "Jingle Bells" or "Frosty the Snowman" each time you enter the classroom?

In gym class, which would you rather do: eat a fruitcake for lunch or compete in a fruitcake throwing contest?

Do you prefer to sing or play an instrument when you participate in the school Christmas program?

Do you like to watch Frosty the Snowman or Rudolph the Red-Nosed Reindeer every day after school?

Which of your closest companions could you rather enjoy Christmas Eve with?

Would you rather have sprinkles on Christmas treats or none at all?

Do you prefer snow on Christmas Day or not any snow at all?

Which do you like better, Santa's beard or his belly?

Do you like to spend special times of year on a homestead or in a major city?

Which one would you prefer: Neither a Christmas tree nor presents

Do you prefer tinsel for your hair or holiday lights for your nails?

Do you prefer to be green like the Grinch or the ears of elves?

Questions for students about Christmas and a break from school

Could you rather go sledding or caroling?
Would you rather wear only red and green to school for a year than respond with "ho ho ho" when someone calls your name?
Do you prefer to sing a solo in the school Christmas program or dance in the Nutcracker?
Do you like to eat one advent chocolate each day, or do you prefer to eat them all at once?
Could you rather have Christmas supper with your family or the President?
Would you rather eat only cookies for a day or hot chocolate?
Do you prefer to spend Christmas Day in a warmer or colder location?
Would you rather watch How the Grinch Stole Christmas or Charlie Brown Christmas?

Which movie do you like to watch the most? The Polar Express or The Nightmare Before Christmas?

When you hit the snooze button, do you want your alarm to play "We Wish You a Merry Christmas" or "12 Days of Christmas"?

For every snack, do you prefer sugar cookies or gingerbread men?

Do you prefer to walk every day to school in snowshoes or elf shoes?

Could you rather spend Christmas at home without anyone else or in New York City without anyone else?

Do you prefer to see the Nutcracker or perform in it?

Would you rather write a holiday story or a poem?

Would you rather read only holiday-themed books for a month or nothing at all?

Questions about winter would you rather

Would you rather take one week off because of snowfall or an additional week of summer vacation?

Work from home or use snowshoes to get to work or school is your choice.

Would you rather have your home so warm that you must wear summer clothes inside or so cold that you must wear a hat and mittens?

Which would you rather construct, an angel or a snowman?

Do you prefer to make soup for your neighbors or help them shovel snow?

Which would you rather eat during the winter— soup for every meal for a week or salad for every meal for a week?

Would you rather consume hot cocoa instead of frozen yogurt for each pastry for a year?

Which would you rather experience, a week without cell service in the snow or Wi-Fi?

Do you prefer to go skiing or read a book in front of the fire?

Which do you prefer, chili or chicken noodle soup?

Do you prefer an oversized sweater or a warm scarf?

Ice fishing or ice skating sound more interesting to you?

Would you rather host a football party or go to a hockey game?

Do you prefer to snowshoe or ride a snowmobile down a mountain?

Do you prefer to take the Polar Bear Plunge or soak in a hot spring?

Winter vacation activity for kids and adults
Which would you rather wear for the day—mittens or wet socks?

Do you prefer to sleep in a snowsuit at night or to sleep in your pajamas during the day?

Do you prefer to play snowball fights or build a snow fort?

Do you prefer a carrot nose or eyes filled with coal?

Do you prefer iced hot chocolate or iced hot apple cider?

Do you prefer to wear earmuffs or a stocking hat?

Do you prefer to sit by the fireplace or wrap yourself in a warm blanket?

Do you prefer fuzzy socks or slippers?

Would you rather spend a week in a house without heating or an igloo?

Do you prefer the Groundhog to not see his shadow until early spring or to see it for six more weeks of the winter?

Do you prefer gloves or mittens?

Would you rather play in the snow in your swimsuit or swim in a snowsuit?

Do you prefer a snowball fight or a water balloon fight?

This winter, do you prefer daily snowfall or none at all?

Would you rather spend the winter in Florida or Minnesota?

Chapter 3

The best would you rather questions for Christmas

Do you prefer to spend Christmas at home and get a lot of presents, or would you rather go to Disneyland and not get any?

Do you prefer to sing Jingle Bells with the right lyrics or Batman Smells?

Do you prefer to make presents for your family or ornaments for your Christmas tree rather than buying them?

Do you prefer a gift or a handmade Christmas card?

Is it pragmatic or sentimental?

Do you prefer to buy a Christmas tree that has already been decorated or cut one down and decorate it yourself?

Which do you prefer, receiving or giving?

Would you rather have a gingerbread house or a gingerbread person?

Have you ever noticed that they have distinct flavors?

Do you prefer to walk or drive through the snow?

Might you at some point rather have egg nog or a hot cocoa?

Which do you prefer, Christmas lunch or dinner?

Do you prefer to shovel the driveway of snow or mow the lawn?

Would you rather have a snow day or double pay?

Which vacation would you prefer, summer or Christmas?

Which do you prefer, Christmas morning or Christmas Eve?

Is it immediate or delayed satisfaction?

The mere thought of a Christmas dinner makes my mouth water. Which do you prefer, a Christmas turkey or a Christmas ham?

Which day of the week do you prefer to work at the mall?

Do you like real Christmas trees better or ones that can be used again?

Do you prefer to send Santa an email or a letter? You have mail, ho, ho!

Do you prefer to receive a gift card or take part in Secret Santa?

Which parade, the Santa parade or the Christmas parade, would you rather watch?

Would you rather spend Christmas at home with your family or go on a week-long vacation?

Do you prefer cookies or candy canes?

Do you prefer to spend Christmas Eve with someone else or at your own home?

Do you prefer to listen to Christmas music on the radio or watch Christmas movies on television?

One of my favorite aspects of Christmas are the carols. Do you prefer a white Christmas or a green Christmas?

Do you prefer the scent of cinnamon or pine needles?

Singing Christmas carols or reading your favorite book would be better ways to spend the holidays.

What are your favorite Christmas carols or books?

Which do you prefer, Christmas cookies or gingerbread?

Would you rather have a white Christmas or a green Christmas?

The idea of a Winter Wonderland is something I adore. Do you prefer snow or a lot of sunshine for Christmas?

Which do you prefer to watch, The Grinch or Elf?

Do you prefer to get a present for Christmas or the money to buy one of your own?

Funny questions from would you rather

What's faster: a gallon of eggnog in 15 seconds or 300 sugar cookies in 15 minutes?

Should you devote two days to cleaning up after a huge Christmas meal or two days to preparing it?

Never again eat candy or play in the snow?

Do you prefer to be one of Santa's workshop elves or a 13-inch, walking, and talking nutcracker?

Do you want to live in a huge gingerbread mansion or build a huge gingerbread mansion?

Is the odor in your hair always turkey or chimney smoke?

Be detained for stealing gifts or pretending to be Santa Claus?

Is your Christmas dinner completely drenched in cranberry sauce or gravy? Never again watch a Christmas movie or drink hot chocolate?

Do you give $1,000 to one individual or to 1,000 individuals?

Do elf ears and Santa's white beard last forever?

Do you want to try stuffing 100 marshmallows into your mouth or soak for six hours in a hot chocolate tub?

Do you want to star in the worst Christmas movie ever made or spend a year playing Mrs. Claus?

only be able to recite lyrics or quotes from Christmas movies or songs?

Or will you never again be able to decorate for the holidays?

Shop for 2,000 gifts or wrap 2,000 gifts.

Is Santa Claus sneezing in your face or do you have reindeer poop on your shoes?

Do you observe Christmas consistently or on a regular basis?

Do you want to sit on Santa's lap and wet your pants or sing Christmas songs to 2 million people by yourself?

Do you prefer candy canes for fingers or gumdrops for eyes?

Do you give your crush a used pair of Christmas socks or a three-year-old fruit cake?

Do you prefer to write about Christmas or read a 2,000-page book about Christmas?

Should you kiss a stranger or a polar bear under the mistletoe?

Are you stuck at the airport on Christmas or have you been accidentally locked out of the mall?

Are you Rudolph with a big, glowing red nose or Santa Claus with a big belly?

Do you get 48 horrible gifts that you can't return or do you have to ring the Salvation Army bell for 48 hours?

Fall into a holly bush or sit on a candy cane that has been sharpened?

Do you have skis for your feet or tinsel for your hair?

Are you going to decorate your Christmas tree with cat food or dirty underwear from another person?

Steal Santa's sleigh or accidentally break the most valuable ornament on the Christmas tree?

During Christmas Day, will 100 people cram into your home, or will you be all by yourself?

be made into a real donkey for a play about the Nativity, or spend an hour loudly singing Jingle Bells in a library?

Do 12 drummers drum or 11 flautists funnel?

Would you rather throw away ten other people's presents or walk barefoot on a mile-long path of Lego blocks to get everything you've ever wanted for Christmas?

Do you intend to knit a sweater from Santa's beard hair or wear a sweater made from Santa's beard hair?

Have antlers that return year after year or be completely covered in fur from head to toe?

Either eat a potato and candy cane sandwich or spend three hours walking around the mall with mistletoe on your head.

Do you want to overcook Christmas cookies or untangle Christmas lights all day?

What happens if you lose all of your gifts or luggage at the airport?

Do you have a carrot nose or the hooves of a reindeer?

Ho, ho, ho! squeal as usual, or in an elf-like high, shrill voice?

Be the only one who gave a present or the only one who did not receive one?

Krampus or the monstrous snowman?

Eggnog with a fruitcake flavor or eggnog with a fruit cake flavor?

Do you have a Christmas tree that talks to you and never stops talking about the tree? Or do you keep a fire going in your fireplace?

Participate in a Nutcracker production or ruin one?

Do you prefer to be trapped in a chimney for four hours or to wear a different ugly Christmas sweater every day for four months?

Is it necessary for you to double-check Santa's "naughty or nice" list?

Make an 80-foot-tall gingerbread man or bake a fruitcake that weighs a ton?

Do you give your grandmother an offensive Christmas card or do you receive one from her?